SPORTS

DAVID ROBINSON

THE ADMIRAL

By R. Conrad Stein

CHILDRENS PRESS ®

CHICAGO

Photo Credits

Cover, ©Brian Drake/SportsLight; 6, ©Brian Drake/Sportschrome
East/West; 9, ©Andy Hayt/Focus On Sports; 10, AP/Wide World;
13, ©Tim DeFrisco/Allsport USA; 14, AP/Wide World; 17, ©Tim
DeFrisco/Allsport USA; 18, 21, UPI/Bettmann; 22, AP/Wide World;
25, 27, UPI/Bettmann; 28, AP/Wide World; 31, ©Brian Drake/
SportsLight; 33, 35, Wide World Photos; 36, Focus On Sports;
37, ©Ken Levine/Allsport USA; 39, Focus On Sports; 40, ©Brian
Drake/SportsLight; 43, ©Brian Drake/Sportschrome East/West;
44, ©Mike Powell/Allsport USA

Project Editor: Shari Joffe
Design: Beth Herman Design Associates
Photo Research: Jan Izzo

Library of Congress Cataloging-in-Publication Data

Stein, R. Conrad.
    David Robinson (the Admiral) / by R. Conrad Stein.
      p. cm. – (Sports stars)
    ISBN 0-516-04382-X
    1. Robinson, David, 1965- –Juvenile literature. 2. Basketball
players–United States–Biography–Juvenile literature. I. Title.
II. Series.
GV884.R615S74   1994
796.323'092–dc20
[B]   93-38039
                                       CIP
                                        AC

Copyright 1994 by Childrens Press®, Inc.
All rights reserved. Published simultaneously in Canada.
Printed in the United States of America.
1 2 3 4 5 6 7 8 9 10 R 03 02 01 00 99 98 97 96 95 94

DAVID ROBINSON

THE ADMIRAL

Not long ago, David Robinson began reading a book called *A Brief History of Time*. It is a fascinating but complex book, written by a great scientist. "He talks about four dimensions and stuff," said David. "How black holes are created. Phenomenal!" Not many people get so excited about a science book. But David Robinson is different from most people.

He plays the piano. Beethoven is his favorite composer. He also plays the saxophone. He likes making up his own jazz tunes. "I'm better on the piano, but with the sax I feel more creative, freer." For enjoyment he tinkers with electronic gadgets. Oh, yes, he also plays basketball for the San Antonio Spurs.

★ ★ ★

On the basketball court, Robinson is different, too. He is a 7-foot, 1-inch center who weighs 235 pounds. Yet he has moves that a 6-foot guard would envy. To get open for a shot, he spins with the grace of a ballet dancer. He runs the floor as if shot from a spring. "He's different from any center in the league," said Larry Brown, his first coach in the pros. "He has unbelievable speed."

Even his background is different from that of most basketball players. Most of Robinson's teammates in the NBA were basketball stars in elementary school and in high school. They went to colleges that were basketball powers. As a boy, David showed only a casual interest in athletics. His college was the United States Naval Academy. There he trained to be an officer onboard a ship.

David clowning around with his younger brother Chuck

David Robinson was born on August 6, 1965. He grew up in Virginia Beach, Virginia, with his younger brother, Chuckie, and his older sister, Kimberly. David's father, Ambrose, was a career man in the U.S. Navy. David's mother was a nurse.

The Robinsons were a happy, loving family. "We knew what was right and wrong," David remembered. "We had responsibilities, but we had freedom, too." All the Robinson children were expected to excel in school. "Once, in junior high school," David said, "I got an A, two B's, and a C, and I was grounded for six weeks because of the C."

Both of David's parents grew up in the South, where they felt the sting of discrimination against African Americans. In the 1950s, when David's father was a high-school student in Arkansas, blacks and whites in the South went to separate public schools. In fact, Arkansas's governor at the time, Orval Faubus, once sent the Arkansas National Guard to all-white Little Rock Central High School to block black students from entering. By contrast, David went to school mostly with white kids. "It never dawned on me I was black," David said of his boyhood.

"David was a normal, curious little boy," said his mother, Freda. "Very perceptive. Always taking things apart to see how they worked." While waiting in supermarket lines with his mother, David developed the habit of rapidly adding up all the items in the cart before they got to the check-out register.

David has always been a well-rounded athlete.

Since David's test scores were in the top percentile, he was placed in the gifted classes. He loved math, and science projects engrossed him. Sports? Sure, they were fun. But he was usually busy doing other things.

When David started high school, he stood 5-foot-5. He joined the basketball team, but then quit because, as he later said, "I really wasn't very good." Still, he was a superb athlete in other areas. He played baseball, he bowled, and he took gymnastics classes. In gymnastics, he learned to walk the length of a basketball court on his hands.

Then he started growing—at the incredible rate of three inches a year. His senior year, he reached 6-foot-6, the same height as his father. His high-school coach could not help noticing this tall, skinny kid walking the halls. He asked David to try out for the team.

In the gym, David dunked the ball in his stocking feet. The coach was astounded. Dunking without gym shoes to provide a grip on the floor required amazing leaping ability. The coach made David the starting center, even though David had little basketball experience.

As a high-school player, David was excellent, but he captured no headlines. Instead of sports, he concentrated on his studies. For years, he had wanted to go to the United States Naval Academy at Annapolis, Maryland. As a navy enlisted man, his father had built a good life for the family. David thought that he would like to go to the academy and strive to become an officer as well. The school accepted him, but not on the basis of his basketball skills. The Naval Academy welcomed him because he was a superior student with high test scores.

David hangs onto the rim after slam-dunking the ball.

David quickly became the star of his college team.

At Annapolis, David became one of 5,000 "midshipmen," the navy's term for student officers. As a "middie," he was roused out of bed at five in the morning and made to march and salute the colors. Drilling and studies meant a 17-hour workday for David and his classmates. David was a member of the basketball team, but the academy did not pamper athletes.

In college, David Robinson kept growing. In less than two years, he shot up to 7-foot-1. He grew so fast that the academy was unable to find uniforms large enough to fit him. Remarkably, the extra inches did not reduce his speed, his quickness, or his gymnastic grace. Instead, the added height gave him the ability to reach two and three feet above the basketball rim. In his sophomore year, he was scoring 20 points a game and sweeping rebounds off the backboards like a human vacuum cleaner.

Sportswriters began drifting into the academy's gym to see this phenomenal new player. The Naval Academy had never been a strong basketball school. It was unusual for sportswriters to visit there. David refused to allow his sudden fame to make him bigheaded. "I never thought of myself as a big-time basketball player," he told one writer. "I still don't. In high school, basketball was something I sort of experimented with. . . . Now, I work hard at it because I think I have the potential to be good. But if I don't become a star, it isn't that much of a deal to me."

David competes for control of a loose ball during a college game.

His reputation as an exceptionally talented college player was established after his second year. Now he faced a tough decision. Upon entering the academy, David had agreed to serve five years as a naval officer after graduation. All Naval Academy students make that pledge. However, if a student decides to leave the academy before his junior year, he or she is no longer obliged to become an officer. There is no dishonor in leaving the school. One-third of all midshipmen drop out or transfer to another school before their junior year.

———— ★ ★ ★ ————

Already, coaches and writers were predicting that David would play professional ball. That meant he would be offered a contract worth thousands, perhaps millions of dollars. But would an NBA team want him after he spent five years in the navy and was older, his basketball skills rusty with disuse? David had long talks with his father. The talks helped him decide whether he should leave or stay at the academy. Finally, David announced that he would stay. He felt he had to pay back the navy for giving him a fine education. As for the money the NBA could offer, he said, "I don't live for money. . . . A lot of people think you are automatically happy if you have a lot of money. I don't necessarily believe that is true."

David is congratulated after being named the nation's top college basketball player in 1987.

Because of Robinson's sparkling play, the Naval Academy became a feared basketball team. In four years, David led the school to an astonishing record of 106 wins against 25 losses. He was the navy's high-powered battleship. They called him "the Admiral."

The navy made an important announcement concerning Midshipman David Robinson during his senior year. Navy authorities now considered David to be too tall for the service. The beds on aircraft carriers and submarines were simply not long enough to accommodate a man of his height. The extra inches he had grown while at the academy disqualified him from sea duty. He would have to serve on a land base for two years, but his five-year obligation was waived.

David celebrates a Navy win.

On the same day that he was picked first in the NBA draft, David visited the White House and met Vice President George Bush.

———————— ★ ★ ★ ————————

In 1987, David Robinson graduated from the Naval Academy. He had carried a B average in a very demanding mathematics program. The same year, the San Antonio Spurs made David the first player picked in the NBA college draft. In choosing David, San Antonio bypassed such talented players as Scottie Pippen, Kevin Johnson, and Horace Grant. Furthermore, the Spurs would have to wait two years for David while he served his hitch in the navy. But Spurs management believed that David was the type of impact player who comes along only once in a decade.

Thousands of excited fans crowded into San Antonio's HemisFair Arena on opening day, 1989. They had come to see the debut of the team's rookie center, who had just been discharged from the United States Navy. The Spurs' first game that year was against the Los Angeles Lakers. The masterful Magic Johnson was the Lakers point guard. Late in the third quarter, Magic drove to the basket for what appeared to be an easy lay up. Then suddenly, like a guided missile, David darted to the painted area to slap Magic's shot out of bounds. The veteran Laker guard shook his head in disbelief. After the game, Magic said, "It's hard to say [Robinson's] a rookie . . . Some guys just aren't ever rookies."

Great centers form the heart of NBA teams. They are big, strong men, like Olajuwon, Ewing, and Cartwright. David was not as strong as the Ewings and the Cartwrights. But no other big man had his catlike hands, his speed, and his tremendous leaping ability.

Even as a rookie, David was noticed by such greats as Magic Johnson. Here the two are shown a few years later, when they played together as members of the 1992 U.S. Olympic "Dream Team."

David's matches with New York Knicks center Patrick Ewing were classics. Ewing was a mountain of muscle. When they faced each other, a story from the Bible came to life: David versus the Goliath. In the closing minutes of one close game, Ewing broke free under the basket. A teammate spotted him and hurled a pass. David Robinson raced the width of the floor to intercept the pass. While falling, he flipped the ball to a teammate who dribbled downcourt to score a Spurs fast-break bucket. "I watched the whole thing, and I still can't believe it," said the Knicks coach. "Robinson was practically on the ground, and he got up in a millisecond to make the steal. . . . I mean he did what most normal human beings can't do."

David playing against Patrick Ewing

Defense. Squads in the NBA live or die by their ability to stop the other guys from scoring. Great defensive play triggers the offense in pro ball. A play that became David's signature won many games for the Spurs. The play is a blur of motion, but it goes roughly like this: David leaps practically through the roof to block a shot, David tears down the court like a sprinter, a teammate lofts a pass, David jams the ball through the hoop down to his elbows. The play amounts to a four-point gain for the Spurs. David denies the opposition two points at one end of the court, while scoring two at the other end. Defense. It wins games in the NBA.

David tears down the court.

In his rookie season, David did for San Antonio what he once did for the Naval Academy. He took a weak team and turned it into a powerhouse. In 1988-89, before Robinson joined the squad, the Spurs had a dismal year, winning 21 games and losing 61. In his rookie season, David helped reverse those numbers to 56 wins against 26 defeats. Not even Michael Jordan had such an immediate impact on his team his first year in the NBA.

Naturally, David had help. He played beside
veterans Terry Cummings and Caldwell Jones.
Providing spark was such young talent as Sean
Elliot and Willie Anderson. This blend of youth
and experience, led by the most explosive center
in the league, promised a bright future for the
San Antonio Spurs.

For his performance that first season, David won the NBA Rookie of the Year award. After that sensational start, he experienced both triumphs and disappointments. Injuries plagued the Spurs in 1990-91, and the team lost their sharpness. The next season, David led the league in blocked shots and was named Defensive Player of the Year. He won the award despite missing the latter part of the season due to thumb surgery. The 1992-93 Spurs were strong early, but faded in the playoffs.

Certainly David's greatest off-the-court triumph came in his third season with the pros, when he married Valerie Hoggatt. The two met in Los Angeles, where Valerie was a student. Teammates Terry Cummings, Sean Elliot, and Avery Johnson were ushers in the wedding party. All guests agreed the ceremony was lovely. But the couple had no time for a honeymoon. David had to fly to Dallas the next day to play the Mavericks.

David is famous for his spectacular defensive play.

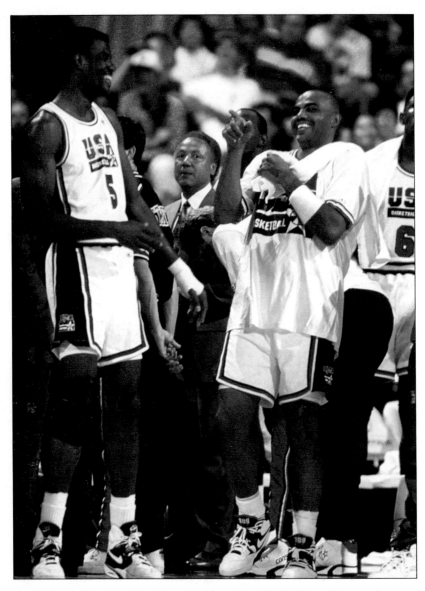

David and Charles Barkley during the 1992 Olympics

David was one of the chosen few to join the greatest basketball team ever assembled, the 1992 U.S. Olympic Team. Nicknamed the Dream Team, it was truly a cavalcade of stars. Its members included Michael Jordan, Scottie Pippen, Charles Barkley, Magic Johnson, and Larry Bird. David's appearance at the 1992 Summer Games was his second at the Olympics. Four years earlier, while serving in the navy, he had been a member of the U.S. Olympic team that went to Seoul, South Korea. That team, made up of young college players, was able to grab only a third-place bronze medal. In 1992, the pros were allowed to compete. The Dream Team swept through its opposition by an average of 50 points a game to secure a gold medal for the United States.

In addition to being a famous basketball player, David has a warm smile and an excellent speaking voice. Because of these qualities, a well-known shoe company asked him to act in a series of commercials on television. One commercial is a takeoff on the popular children's show "Mr. Rogers' Neighborhood." In the commercial, David warns people involved with drugs to stay away from "Mr. Robinson's Neighborhood." Says the Spurs center, "Mr. Robinson doesn't want garbage in his neighborhood."

Commercials and basketball have made David Robinson a millionaire. But he readily gives money back to his community. One of his favorite charities grants scholarships to underprivileged San Antonio kids. The director of this charity said, "Apart from the fact that he's a tremendous basketball player, David Robinson is also a tremendous human being."

Millions of fans around the country agree.

Chronology

1965 – David Robinson is born on August 6, 1965, in Key West, Florida. His father, Ambrose, is a navy career man, and his mother, Freda, is a nurse. David grows up in Virginia Beach, Virginia.

1979 – As a freshman at Green Run High School in Virginia Beach, David stands 5-foot-5. He makes the basketball team, but quits because he spends most of his time on the bench. He plays baseball, bowls, and runs track. But mostly, he concentrates on his studies. He is determined to attend college at the U.S. Naval Academy, where excellent grades are demanded from every student.

1982 – David's family moves, and David begins his senior year at Osbourn Park High School in Manassas, Virginia. He has grown to 6-foot-6. The coach at Osbourn Park asks him to try out for basketball, and he quickly becomes the team's starting center.

1983 – Robinson enters the Naval Academy at Annapolis, Maryland, as a midshipman. He joins the academy's basketball team.

1985 – David's second year at the Naval Academy is
phenomenal. He scores an average of 23.6 points
per game and grabs 11.6 rebounds per game.
He leads a relatively weak Navy team to the
NCAA Tourney.

– At the end of his second year, David faces a difficult
decision. He can transfer to another college and seek
a pro contract when he graduates, or he can stay with
the Naval Academy. If he stays, he will have to serve
five years as a navy officer when he graduates. David
decides to remain at the academy.

1986 – Once more, David leads the Naval Academy team to
the NCAA playoffs.

1987 – David's last year in college is his best. He averages
28.2 points per game.

– The navy announces that Robinson's height (now 7-foot-1)
makes him too tall to work on navy ships; therefore he
will have to serve only two years as a navy officer instead
of the usual five.

– David becomes the first player chosen in the NBA college
draft. He is picked by the San Antonio Spurs.

1989 – David starts with the Spurs after completing his service in the navy.

1990 – David wins the NBA Rookie of the Year award.

1992 – An injured thumb causes David to miss the latter part of the 1991-92 season, but he is still named NBA Defensive Player of the Year.
  – David becomes a member of the Dream Team—the 1992 U.S. Olympic men's basketball team. At the Summer Olympics in Barcelona, Spain, the Dream Team crushes its opposition on the way to winning a gold medal.

1993 – The Spurs, led by Robinson, enjoy a strong regular season in 1992-93, but fade in the playoffs.

★ ★ ★

About the Author

In his youth, Mr. Stein was a mediocre basketball player, a poor baseball player, and an absolute disaster as a football player. Consequently, he spent many hours on the sidelines of athletic fields watching more gifted athletes perform. From an early age he became a fan.

Mr. Stein is the author of many books, articles, and short stories for young people. He lives in Chicago with his wife and their daughter Janna.

West Side Christian School
Library